Pup and Hound Move In

For Emily and Allison — S.H.
For Little Sid — L.H.

Kids Can Read™ Kids Can Read is a trademark of Kids Can Press Ltd.

Text © 2004 Susan Hood
Illustrations © 2004 Linda Hendry

Kids Can Press acknowledges the financial support of the
Government of Ontario, through the Ontario Media Development
Corporation's Ontario Book Initiative; the Ontario Arts Council; the
Canada Council for the Arts; and the Government of Canada,
through the BPIDP, for our publishing activity.

. ʾblished in Canada by   Published in the U.S. by
h ⸀ls Can Press Ltd.   Kids Can Press Ltd.
29 Birch Avenue   2250 Military Road
Toronto, ON M4V 1E2   Tonawanda, NY 14150

www.kidscanpress.com

The artwork in this book was rendered in pencil crayons
on a siena colored pastel paper.
The text is set in Bookman.

Edited by Tara Walker
Designed by Julia Naimska
Printed in China by WKT Company Limited

The hardcover edition of this book is smyth sewn casebound.
The paperback edition of this book is limp sewn with a
drawn-on cover.

CM 04 0 9 8 7 6 5 4 3 2 1
CM PA 04 0 9 8 7 6 5 4 3 2 1   0565

National Library of Canada Cataloguing in Publication Data

Hood, Susan

Pup and hound move in / Susan Hood ; illustrated by Linda Hendry.

(Kids Can read)

ISBN 1-55337-674-9 (bound).   ISBN 1-55337-675-7 (pbk.)

1. Dogs — Juvenile fiction. I. Hendry, Linda II. Title. III. Series: Kids
Can read (Toronto, Ont.)

PZ7.H758Pup 2004   j813'.54   C2004-900112-4

Kids Can Press is a corus™ Entertainment company

Pup and Hound
Move In

Written by Susan Hood

Illustrated by Linda Hendry

Kids Can Press

What was that?

What woke Hound up?

It was near dawn —

Yawn!

What woke Hound up?

It was Pup!

Pup came over

every day.

"Woof! Woof!" he'd say.

"Come out and play!"

They played follow-the-leader
and tug-of-war.

And Hound wasn't lonely

anymore.

At night, Pup went home

to his old boot bed.

He wished he was

somewhere else instead.

Pup didn't want

to live alone.

So he left with

everything he owned.

His good friend Hound
took him in
and promised to
take care of him.

But the day Pup moved in,

he took Hound's bone.

Groan!

He ate Hound's food.

How rude!

He slept in Hound's bed!

Sleepyhead!

16

Hound stretched out on

the hard wood floor.

And then — oh, no!

That puppy snored!

When Hound woke up,

Pup wasn't there.

Hound found him

with his special bear.

Pup was teething,

as puppies do.

He needed to chew

and chew and chew!

Hound grabbed his bear.

And Pup did, too.

They pulled and pulled!

Bear split in two!

The pigs and cows
stopped to stare.
They knew it was
Hound's special bear.

Even the donkeys

looked up from their hay.

Hound sighed, turned

and walked away.

25

Pup heard a howl,

a low, sad song.

Other dogs heard

and howled along.

Pup crept up the hill
without a sound.
He gave his
lucky sock to Hound.

Then Pup howled, too,

"*Ah-rut-ah-roooooooooooo!*"

It sounded so funny,

what could Hound do?

Hound wagged his tail.

Pup wagged his, too.

Then Hound found something
for Pup to chew.